Who Stole My Leg?
Somos8 Series

© Text: José Carlos Andrés, 2013
© Illustrations: Myriam Cameros Sierra, 2013
© Edition: NubeOcho, 2022
© Translation: Robin Sinclair, 2019
www.nubeocho.com · hello@nubeocho.com

Original Title: *El pirata de la pata de pata*
Design: Isabel de la Sierra
Color correction: José Moya
Text editing: Cecilia Ross, Caroline Dookie and Rebecca Packard

First edition: June 2022
ISBN: 978-84-17673-65-9
Legal deposit: M-10099-2021

Printed in Portugal.

WHO STOLE MY LEG?

JOSÉ CARLOS ANDRÉS
MYRIAM CAMEROS SIERRA

nubeOCHO

GRISLYGRIN

was **the scariest** pirate
of the **Seven Seas** of all **time.**

He was **so scary**
that he didn't even shave
so that he wouldn't have to see
his reflection in the mirror.

If he did, he would

SCARE HIMSELF.

Dry Desert
Mosquitoes

Cape
Tuna
Flies

spent most of his time
IN HIS CABIN...

CLONK

But every time he went
for a walk on the ship deck,

the **clonk, clonk, clonk**

of his wooden pegleg would make
his crew scream in **fear**.

They were all **afraid** of him...

AAAAAH

One night,
a little freckled cabin girl
decided to sneak into **Grislygrin's**
cabin while he was

ASLEEP.

She stole his
wooden pegleg
and swapped it for
a squeaky
RUBBER DUCK.

The next morning, after having a **whole shark** for breakfast, **Grislygrin** went for a walk on the ship's deck...

The wicked pirate
slipped and banged his
nose against the mainmast.
It swelled up and turned
as purple as a **plum.**

QUAACK

The following night, while the captain was sleeping, **a little cabin boy** was the only one brave enough to sneak into **Grislygrin's** cabin.

He swapped the captain's **squeaky rubber leg** for a

SPRING.

After having **twelve pounds of sea urchins** for breakfast, **Grislygrin** went to the ship's deck to get some fresh air...

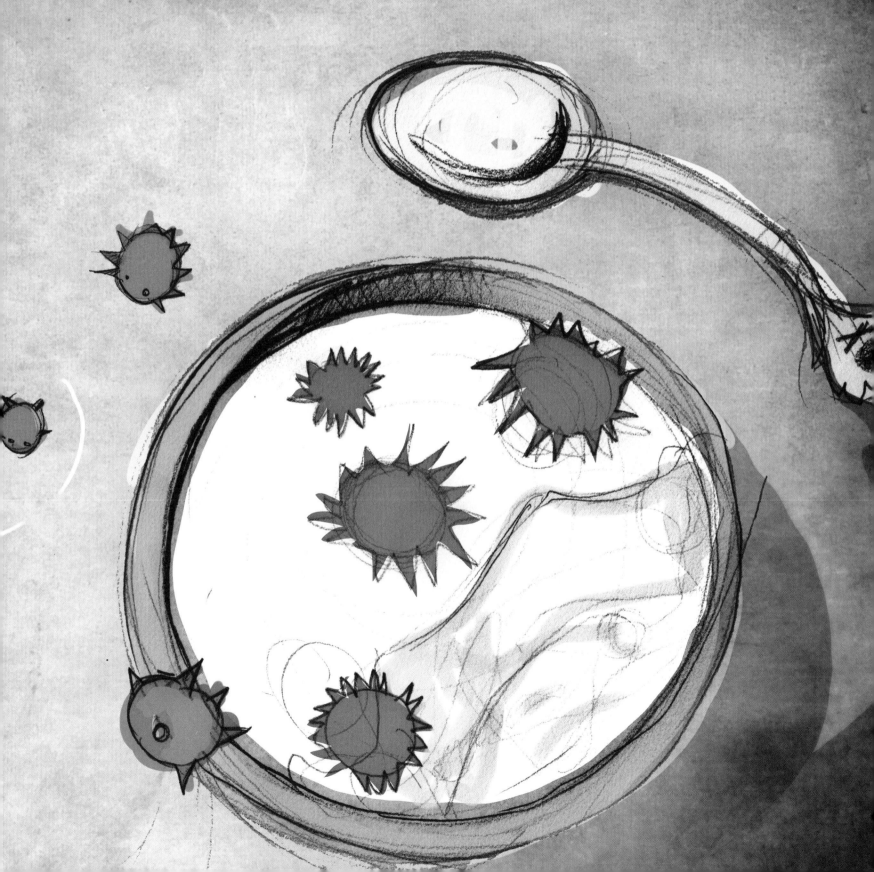

Boing, **boing**, **boing**...
**Grislygrin started bouncing
like a basketball!**

BOING

The ship went over **a huge wave**
and the captain **bounced** and bounced
so high that he nearly fell into the water.

After dinner, **two twin brothers** decided to creep into **Grislygrin's** cabin while he was sleeping.

They swapped his spring leg for... for... **for a dog!**
Yes, a **dog**! A big hairy

DOG.

When the captain got up, he couldn't even get dressed, because the dog was pulling him to the deck to go pee on the **mainmast.**

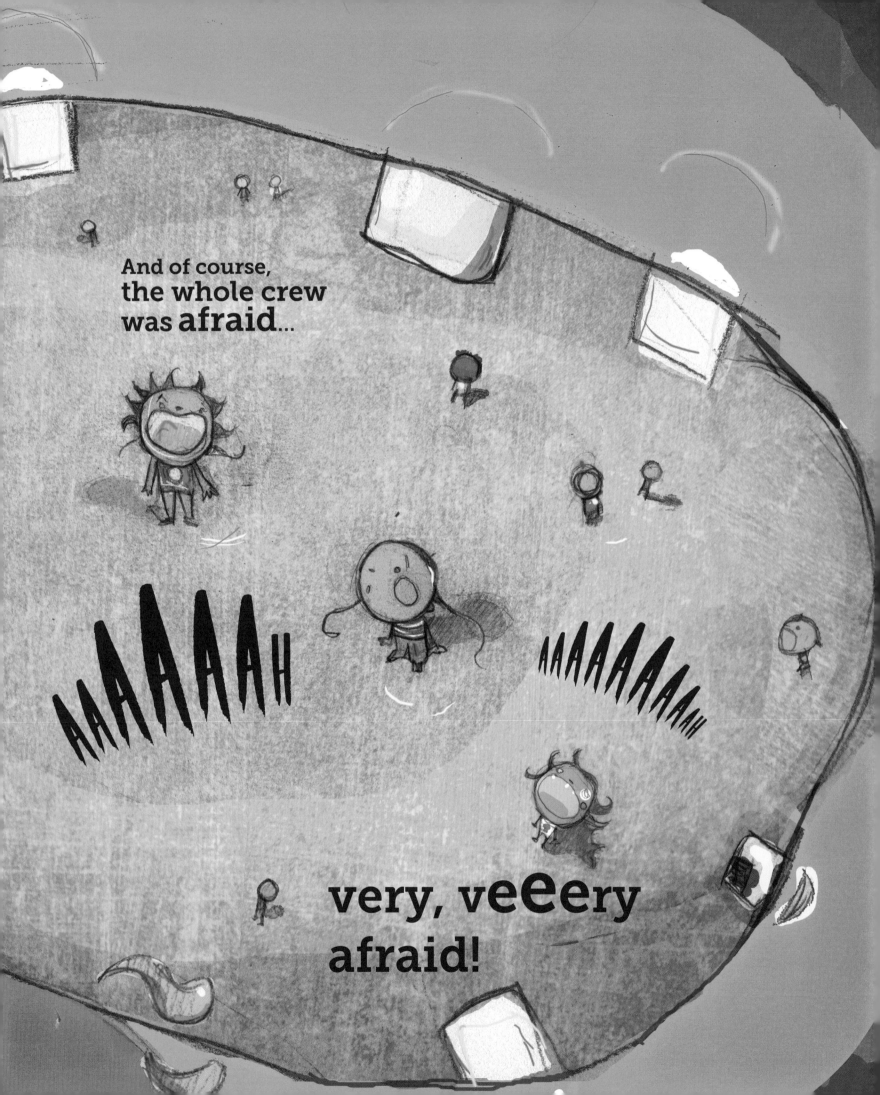

Tired of being so
scared all the time,
the **smallest cabin girl of all**
sneaked into **Grislygrin's** cabin
and swapped his dog leg for... **for...**

You'd better turn the page and see
with your own
EYES...

The next morning,
after having a **jellyfish** salad
and two dozen fish bones,
Grislygrin went to the ship's deck.

"There once was a pirate, **the scariest pirate** of the Seven Seas of all time,"

his **LEG**

wrote.

Every time the **captain walked,**

HIS PENCIL LEG

drew and wrote stories and adventures of enormous whales and hidden treasures.

Ever since that day, the crew
was no longer afraid of **Grislygrin**.
And everynight, before going to sleep,
they would ask him to take long walks
on the deck so they could listen to his

WONDERFUL PIRATE TALES.